Anna & Elsa

The Great Ice Engine

For Dana Felkoff Kennedy,
may you always face forward.
—E.D.

rhcbooks.com

Box ISBN 978-0-7364-4092-9

Printed in the United States of America
10 9 8 7 6 5 4 3 2 1

Disney
Anna & Elsa

The Great
Ice Engine

By Erica David
Illustrated by Bill Robinson,
Manuela Razzi, Francesco Legramandi,
and Gabriella Matta

Random House 🏠 New York

Chapter 1

Mornings in Arendelle ran like clockwork. The scent of freshly baked bread drifted from the bakeries. The delicious smell started a chain reaction. It woke the children, who woke their parents, who went to the market to buy the bread to fill their bellies and start the day.

In the castle, Anna and Elsa also woke to the smell of bread baking. They followed the wonderful scent into the kitchen. There, the castle chef was waiting for them with two small loaves of bread fresh from the oven.

"Good morning, ladies," he greeted them.

"Good morning," said Elsa and Anna.

The chef wrapped the warm loaves in handkerchiefs and handed them to Anna and Elsa. Today the sisters were visiting the busy market square—they would take their breakfast with them. Elsa and Anna thanked the chef. They gathered their cloaks and set out for town.

As they walked through the village, they saw the market come alive. Merchants opened their shops and set out their wares. It was officially time for the day to begin.

Anna and Elsa passed a line of villagers waiting to buy ice. Ice was important to the kingdom of Arendelle, especially during the warm summer months. The townspeople used it to keep food fresh and themselves cool.

Even though Elsa could form ice with her special powers, she only used her powers for emergencies. Arendelle's ice was supplied by the ice harvesters, who worked high in the mountains. Every morning, they delivered ice to the castle and the town.

As the sisters approached the square, they noticed a crowd of people gathering along the edge of the market.

"I wonder what's going on," said Elsa.

"Let's find out," Anna replied.

They hurried across the busy square. By the time they reached the other side, the crowd had grown twice as thick.

"I can't see a thing!" Anna exclaimed. She hopped up and down and peered between the villagers' heads.

"Easy, there, jumping bean," Elsa said. She gently tapped a tall man standing in front of her. "Excuse me, sir, do you mind if we come through?"

The man smiled at Elsa and stepped aside. "Make way for Her Majesty!" he called. The villagers parted, clearing a path for Elsa and Anna. The sisters found their way through the group of townspeople.

When they reached the front of the

crowd, Elsa gasped. Sitting on a cart in front of her was the strangest contraption she'd ever seen. It was a huge barrel, open on one side. It was filled with all sorts of odds and ends, including a moldy wedge of cheese. There were pulleys, levers, chutes, and gears. A wooden wheel with an old snowshoe attached sat beneath a bucket full of what looked like marbles, and a puff of steam belched from a rusty food tin.

"What in the world . . . ?" Elsa said.

Anna blinked, fascinated. "Is that a goat horn?" she asked, pointing to one of the machine's many parts.

"Hoo-hoo!" cried a friendly voice.

A tall, barrel-chested man with a reddish-blond beard greeted them. It was Oaken, the owner of Wandering Oaken's Trading Post & Sauna. He placed a hand proudly on the strange device. "May I introduce . . . my latest invention!"

"Wow. That's amazing, Oaken!" Anna

said. She stared at it for another moment. "What is it?"

"It's the best thing since Jarlsberg cheese!" Oaken answered.

"Uh-huh. What is it?" Anna asked again.

"It will change the face of Arendelle forever!"

"Right, but what is it? The suspense is killing me!" Anna said excitedly.

"An ice engine," Oaken announced, beaming with pride.

"Oh. I see," Anna replied. But she didn't really. She looked to Elsa for an answer. Elsa shrugged. She was just as puzzled as her sister.

"It cuts the ice, *ja?*" Oaken explained.

The crowd of villagers looked equally baffled. They murmured to each other in confusion. Oaken's ice engine was clearly handmade. Wooden planks had been haphazardly nailed together, and several parts were attached with shoestrings. One gear looked like it was held in place by chewing gum. Overall, the machine looked very unsteady. It didn't look like it could cut bread, let alone ice.

"I come from a long line of inventors," Oaken said. "Maybe you've heard of my great-uncle Jarl?"

"I don't think so," Elsa said.

"He's famous for inventing the Heifersling," Oaken told them.

Elsa and Anna looked at Oaken blankly.

"It is only the greatest cow-carrying device known to man!" boasted Oaken.

"Right," Anna said. "Um, why do we need to carry cows?"

"To move them from place to place," Oaken replied.

"Couldn't you just herd them?" Anna asked.

"Why herd them when you can carry them? Much nicer for the cows, *ja?*"

Curious, Elsa walked around the cart. She studied the ice engine from every angle. "How did you come up with this, Oaken?" she asked.

"Funny story," Oaken said. "I was sitting in my shop after my big blowout sale. I had so many items left over—snowshoes, ropes, food tins. I thought, 'Oaken, you should make something with these items, *ja?*'" Oaken smiled. He gazed off into the distance as if reliving a beloved childhood memory.

"So I gathered everything together and began to build," he continued. "I had no idea what I was making. But after an hour or two, I had made an ice cutter!" Oaken clapped his hands delightedly. "I thought, 'Oaken, Great-Uncle Jarl is so proud of you.'"

"That's a wonderful story, Oaken," Elsa said. "But the ice harvesters have been cutting ice by hand for years."

"I know this," Oaken said. "They are always buying boots and saws and ropes and pickaxes from my store. They are my best customers. I thought, 'Hoo-hoo, Oaken, you can help the harvesters.'"

Anna squinted at the ice engine. She had no idea how it worked. "Maybe you could give us a demonstration," she said.

"Yes, that was my plan," Oaken told them. "I was going to the frozen lake in the mountains to try it out. But this crowd of curious onlookers stopped me. I thought, 'Oaken, you must tell these people about your invention.'"

"Well, you've told us," Anna said.

"Just so," Oaken replied. "And now, if you will follow me, I will *show* you."

Chapter 2

Oaken led his horse-drawn cart high into the mountains. Elsa, Anna, and the crowd of curious onlookers followed. When they reached the frozen lake, they saw Kristoff and the ice harvesters hard at work. The men and women sang happily as they cut the ice into perfect blocks.

"Hoo-hoo, harvesters!" Oaken called in greeting. The ice harvesters put down their long saws and waved hello. They welcomed everyone to the lake.

"That's quite the machine there, Oaken. What does it do?" asked Stellan, one of the harvesters.

"Allow me to give you a demonstration," Oaken answered. He carefully pushed his cart out onto the ice. The ice harvesters and the villagers drew closer to get a better look.

Oaken checked the machine's parts. He tested the pulleys and sniffed the moldy cheese.

As Oaken prepared his invention, Kristoff walked over to Anna and Elsa.

"Is that a goat horn?" he whispered.

"That's what *I* said!" Anna told him.

Kristoff looked the ice engine up and down. "Hmm. Doesn't look like much," he said.

"It does seem a little strange at first glance," Elsa admitted. "But you can't judge anything just by looks."

"I guess so," Kristoff replied. "It's just that I've never seen anything quite so odd."

"This coming from the guy who was raised by trolls," Anna said, chuckling.

"My upbringing was perfectly normal," Kristoff replied.

Anna knew that Kristoff had a point. What was normal for him might seem odd to someone else. The same was true for Oaken and his machine—to Oaken, it probably seemed perfectly normal.

"Anna, do you remember the Cat-a-Cleaner?" Elsa asked.

"Of course!" Anna said. It was one of the happy times she could remember from when they were little, before Elsa accidentally hurt Anna with her magic. They'd invented the Cat-a-Cleaner to quickly clean Anna's room. . . .

Five-year-old Anna knew she had to pick up her toys, but there were so many other things she'd rather do! Adventure awaited her—if she could only clean her room.

"Do I have to, Elsa?" Anna asked dramatically. Her arms were full of stuffed

animals. She tottered unsteadily toward the open toy chest.

"Yes, Anna," eight-year-old Elsa replied. She was helping her little sister clean. Toys were scattered all over the place. By the end of the day, Anna's room always looked like it had been struck by a tornado.

"But can't I do it later?" Anna asked hopefully. It was snowing outside her window. She was eager to go out and play.

Elsa looked at the fluffy polar bears stacked in Anna's arms. "If you put your toys away now, you won't have to do it later," she said brightly. "Besides, Mama said once you're finished, we can go play in the snow."

"Okay," Anna replied. Cleaning wasn't her favorite thing, but if it meant she could go outside, she'd gladly do it. Anna dropped the stuffed animals into the toy chest. She bent down to pick up more toys. "I just wish there was a faster way to do this."

Elsa picked up a pair of ice skates and put them in the wardrobe. "Maybe there is," she said. "I think I have an idea."

Anna perked up. Elsa always had the best ideas. "What is it?" she asked eagerly.

"What if we make something that'll clean your room?" said Elsa.

"Like a snowman?" Anna asked, excited.

"I don't think snowmen are the best room cleaners," Elsa replied. "I was thinking more like some kind of invention."

Anna nodded enthusiastically. "So how do we do it?"

Elsa scratched her chin in thought. She looked around the room and noticed an old jump rope abandoned in a corner. She picked it up and handed it to Anna. "Here, hold this. I'll be right back."

Elsa disappeared into the hallway. A few minutes later she returned, dragging a small teeter-totter and a bucket of stones from the courtyard.

"Elsa, we're supposed to put the toys away, not bring more in!" Anna said playfully.

"These aren't toys, Anna. They're part of our invention," Elsa replied. She moved the teeter-totter into place across from the toy chest. Then she attached the bucket of stones to one end. The teeter-totter dipped under the weight of the bucket. One end sank lower while the other sprang up.

"That end's too heavy, Elsa," Anna said, pointing to the bucket.

"I know," Elsa replied. "But watch this." She pushed her end of the seesaw down, raising the heavy bucket into the air. "Hand me that rope," she said to Anna.

Anna gave her sister the jump rope. Elsa looped it around her end of the teeter-totter to fasten it in place.

"Do I get to seesaw?" Anna asked.

"Not you—them," Elsa answered, pointing to the toys on the floor. She picked up a doll and placed it on her end of the seesaw. "When I say go, you pull the rope. Okay, Anna?"

Anna nodded.

"One . . . two . . . three . . . go!" Elsa said.

Anna yanked the rope and it fell from the seesaw. The bucket of rocks was much heavier than the doll. It plunged toward the ground, flinging the doll into air. The doll sailed across the room and landed in the toy chest. *Thunk!*

"Whoa!" Anna exclaimed. "She flew!"

Elsa nodded.

"It's like a . . . like a . . . cata . . . what's that thing called?" asked Anna.

"A catapult?" said Elsa.

"Yeah, it's like a catapult—only, it cleans my room!" Anna said. Elsa reset the seesaw and helped her sister launch another toy.

Anna giggled delightedly. "It's a Cat-a-Cleaner!" she said. Suddenly, cleaning up didn't seem so bad.

Back in the present, Elsa and Anna shared a laugh.

"The Cat-a-Cleaner, eh? You wouldn't happen to still have it, would you?" Kristoff asked.

Elsa shook her head. "Why?"

"Well, *someone* I know is a messy eater." Kristoff nodded toward his reindeer, Sven. Sven was munching on a carrot just a few feet away. The reindeer left carrot bits everywhere! "Maybe I could use the Cat-a-Cleaner to launch crumbs into a trash can," Kristoff said.

Sven overheard and snorted in disapproval. *"Speak for yourself,"* Kristoff responded in his Sven voice.

"Hoo-hoo! Is everyone ready?" Oaken called.

Anna, Elsa, and Kristoff moved closer to Oaken and the machine. The crowd murmured eagerly. The demonstration was about to begin.

Chapter 3

Oaken made a couple of last-minute adjustments to his invention. First, he opened a small door in the compartment beneath the giant, rusty food tin. The compartment was like a furnace. Oaken stuck his hand inside to test for heat. Satisfied, he shut the door. Next, he pulled a small mouse from the pocket of his sweater. He petted the mouse gently.

Then he placed it inside a small metal wheel.

"I present to you my ice engine!" Oaken announced.

Oaken gave the ship's wheel a mighty spin. That started a chain reaction. The snowshoe attached to the wheel kicked the bucket of marbles. The bucket tipped, and the marbles spilled into a trough. The marbles zigzagged along the trough into another bucket waiting below.

The second bucket was attached by rope to a pulley. On the other end of the rope was the wedge of moldy cheese. As the second bucket filled with marbles, it sank to the ground. The bucket's weight pulled the cheese into the air!

The cheese dangled above the metal wheel with the mouse inside. When the mouse smelled the cheese, it began to run. The wheel spun madly.

Elsa's eyes darted here and there, following the action. There was so much going on, it was hard to keep track!

The mouse's wheel was connected to a

set of gears. The wheel turned the gears, and the gears tripped a lever. The lever opened and closed a hatch in the coal barrel. Each time the hatch opened, a piece of coal fell into a chute. The chute led to the warm furnace beneath the giant, rusty food tin.

"I think I'm getting dizzy!" Anna said.

The mouse chased the cheese. The gears spun. The hatch opened and closed. Coal fell into the chute, but nothing else seemed to happen.

"Is this thing gonna cut ice?" Kristoff asked, amused.

A few nervous giggles escaped from the crowd of ice harvesters and villagers.

They felt embarrassed for Oaken. What if his machine didn't work?

One of the villagers looked almost frightened. He covered his eyes with his hands and peeked worriedly through his fingers. It was Norvald the milliner. He was known for making fancy hats for everyone in town. But he was also known for worrying. The villagers had given him the nickname Nervous Norvald.

"What if the machine explodes?" Norvald whispered to the woman standing next to him.

"Don't worry," she said soothingly.

Norvald looked like his stomach was tied in knots, but Oaken didn't seem worried at all. He waited patiently, confident that all would be well.

After a few minutes, Anna heard a strange bubbling sound.

"What is that?" she asked.

"It sounds like water boiling," answered Elsa.

Sure enough, water was boiling in the giant food tin. A stream of steam escaped through the goat horn attached to the top. It blew a long, loud note, like an angry trumpet.

On the side of the rusty tin, an iron rod pumped in and out. The rod was connected to a metal arm. The arm worked a flywheel, and the wheel turned a pole. At the end of the pole was a sharp saw blade. The blade sank into the ice.

"*Oooooh,*" the crowd gasped.

The pole moved up and down, rotating to cut in a perfect circle. When the circle was complete, a block of ice bobbed on the water beneath.

Kristoff stared in disbelief.

Oaken led the horse-drawn cart forward to a new patch of ice. In less than a minute, his invention had cut five whole blocks!

A few minutes later, Oaken removed the mouse from the wheel. He rewarded it with a piece of cheese. The engine's gears stopped spinning. Eventually, the blade ground to a stop.

The crowd applauded. The ice harvesters were impressed. They looked at the ice carved by Oaken's invention.

Kristoff led the inspection. "The shape is different," he said, pointing. "They look like ice . . . circles."

"Cylinders, *ja?*" Oaken said. Because the engine's blade moved in a circle, the ice blocks it made were round.

"I've never thought of round ice blocks," Stellan the ice harvester said. "I wonder how we could use those."

"How exactly does the engine work, Oaken?" Anna asked.

"Hoo-hoo! I thought you'd never ask!" he replied. Oaken explained that his invention was powered by steam. It needed heat and water. The water was kept in the rusty food tin. The heat came from the furnace beneath.

Oaken had lit a small fire in the furnace before he went to town. By the time he reached the lake, the heat had begun to build. When the coal was added, the fire grew. The heat built up and boiled the water in the tin.

Steam rose from the boiling water. Some of it escaped through the horn in the tin. That made the trumpet sound. The rest of the steam powered the piston. The piston was the metal rod connected to the fly wheel. The wheel worked the pole and the blade.

"Wow," Anna said, impressed.

"It's like a train engine," Elsa added.

"Exactly," Oaken replied, beaming. "Only, a train does not have my little friend Lars here." Oaken nodded to the little gray mouse in his hand. He tucked Lars back into the breast pocket of his sweater. Lars's head poked out of the pocket. He squeaked happily.

"Well, that's great, Oaken. This engine is a doozy, no question," Kristoff said. "But something tells me it's no substitute for a real, live ice harvester." He flexed his muscles playfully. "Am I right?" he asked his fellow ice workers.

The harvesters stared at him blankly.

"Aw, come on, guys. You think this machine can beat us?" he asked.

35

There was no reply.

"Maybe a friendly contest, *ja?*" Oaken said. "You versus the ice engine?"

"You're on!" Kristoff said good-naturedly. "I'll show you just what one man and his trusty saw can do."

"Uh-oh," Anna whispered to Elsa. She glanced at Kristoff, who was puffed up with pride. "Why do I get the feeling that one man and his saw can cause a whole lot of trouble?"

Chapter 4

The next morning, Kristoff arrived at the castle bright and early. He and Oaken had agreed to hold the contest in three days. Kristoff planned to spend those three days training. Anna and Elsa had agreed to help.

"Hey there, Kristoff!" said a familiar voice. Olaf the snowman bounded toward him as he entered the castle.

"Hi, Olaf," Kristoff said. "What are you doing here?"

"I heard all about Oaken's snow-cone machine!" Olaf said. "I've always wanted to try a snow cone! They sound delicious!"

"Uh, Olaf," Kristoff said. "It's not a snow-cone machine. It's an ice engine. It cuts ice blocks—er, circles . . . cylinders."

"Oh, you mean you're not going to practice making snow cones with Elsa and Anna?" Olaf asked.

"No, I'm going to practice my ice-cutting technique with Elsa and Anna," Kristoff replied.

"But you cut ice every day. Why practice that?" said Olaf.

Kristoff sighed patiently. "Because I'm

in training," he explained. "I'm going to get faster and stronger. I'm going to beat that machine."

"Oh," Olaf said again. He was quiet for a moment. Then he said brightly, "Well, if you need a workout buddy, I'm your snowman!"

"You?" Kristoff asked, surprised.

"Of course. How do you think I got this perfect figure?" said Olaf. He rubbed his round snowball belly. "You think I was just made this way?"

*

A short while later, Kristoff, Olaf, Elsa, and Anna were in the ballroom. The large space had been turned into a training gym.

". . . one hundred seventy-one, one hundred seventy-two, one hundred seventy-three . . . ," Anna counted. She was coaching Kristoff through some weightlifting exercises. But instead of lifting weights, Kristoff was lifting Olaf! He pressed the snowman over his head as if he were a barbell.

"Faster!" Anna shouted.

Kristoff picked up the pace. Sweat beaded on his forehead.

"*Wheeeeeeee!*" Olaf said excitedly.

"You know, you're surprisingly heavy for someone made out of snow," Kristoff told him.

Anna continued to count: ". . . one hundred eighty-five, one hundred eighty-six, one hundred eighty-seven . . ."

Kristoff's arms were getting tired. He was out of breath. He began to slow down.

"Come on, you can do it!" Elsa yelled encouragingly.

Kristoff gritted his teeth as if he were calling on every ounce of strength he had left. Olaf cheered him on.

". . . one hundred ninety-eight, one

hundred ninety-nine, and . . . two hundred!" Anna said. "Good job. You can take a break."

Kristoff put Olaf down. Then he collapsed on the floor, panting.

After a moment, Elsa offered him a cool glass of water. Kristoff sat up. He took the water and drank it down in one long gulp.

Olaf looked proud of Kristoff. He opened his twig arms wide. "Warm hug?" he offered.

"Warm hug for you. Cool hug for me," Kristoff said. He was sweating. They hugged, and Kristoff sighed in relief. Then he collapsed onto the floor again.

"Don't tell me you're tired," Anna teased him.

"Hey, you try lifting a snowman over your head two hundred times in a row," Kristoff said.

"That's just the beginning," Anna said. "We still have the obstacle course to go."

"Obstacle course?" Kristoff asked, raising an eyebrow.

Anna and Elsa nodded.

"There's nothing like an obstacle course to build strength and stamina," Elsa explained.

"I tried it out this morning," said Anna. "It works great."

Kristoff climbed to his feet. He mopped the sweat from his forehead. "All right," he said, determined. "Let's do this."

The obstacle course was set up in the castle courtyard. It had four sections: the wagon-wheel run, the mud crawl, the climbing net, and the wall.

"This looks like fun!" Olaf said enthusiastically.

"Easy for you to say," Kristoff told him. The snowman was strapped comfortably to Kristoff's back. Anna had thought it would be more challenging if Kristoff carried some extra weight.

"Is everyone ready?" Elsa asked. She was holding a pocket watch to time Kristoff's run.

"You bet we are!" Olaf answered.

Kristoff nodded firmly.

"Ready, set, go!" Elsa shouted.

Kristoff took off running. He headed straight for the long stretch of wagon wheels. They had been placed flat on the ground, side by side in pairs. He had to run through them without touching the spokes or the sides.

"Knees up!" Anna called encouragingly.

Kristoff jogged through the wheels, lifting his knees high. Olaf bounced up and down gleefully with each step.

"Almost there!" Olaf said.

Kristoff hurried through the last of the wagon wheels. He turned and rushed toward the large mud pit at the edge of the courtyard.

There were ropes strung across the pit a

foot off the ground. The only way to cross the pit was to crawl under the ropes.

Kristoff dropped to his belly. He inched his way forward into the mud. It squished and squelched beneath him.

"Is this really necessary?" he complained. "There's no mud on the frozen lake."

"I'm sorry, did you say that you wanted to win the contest or that you wanted to keep clean?" Anna teased.

Kristoff grumbled and kept crawling. He was halfway through the pit when Olaf's voice rang out. "Lower, please!" The snowman was in danger of getting tangled in the ropes.

Kristoff sank lower. As soon as he opened his mouth to complain, it was filled with mud. *"Blech!"* he said, spitting it out.

"One minute, forty-nine seconds!" Elsa called, keeping track of the time.

Finally, Kristoff reached the end of the mud pit. He got to his feet and ran straight for the climbing net. The net was attached to the castle wall. He had to climb up, touch the top of the wall, and then climb down.

Kristoff jumped onto the net and started to climb. He looked good at first, but he was clearly beginning to tire.

"You can do it!" Elsa shouted.

"Come on, Kristoff!" Olaf cheered. "Think of all the delicious hot chocolate you can have when you're done!"

"Cold chocolate!" Kristoff said, sweating. "I want cold chocolate!"

"Two minutes and fifty-two seconds!" Elsa said.

Kristoff touched the top of the wall. He climbed down and approached the end of the course.

The final obstacle was a six-foot wooden wall with a rope attached. All Kristoff had to do was use the rope to pull himself over. That was easier said than done, however. He was losing steam. He stopped in front of the wall, panting.

Anna could see that Kristoff was exhausted. "Dig deep!" she said. "Don't give up!" She began to clap to show her support. Elsa clapped, too, cheering him on. Even Olaf, riding on Kristoff's back, clapped his tree branch hands.

Kristoff straightened his shoulders. He stared at the wall doggedly. He was determined to finish. He took a deep breath and ran.

Kristoff grabbed the rope, hoisted himself up, and threw himself over the wall. The landing wasn't pretty, but he'd done it! He lay facedown on the courtyard stones, breathing heavily. Both he and Olaf were covered from head to toe in mud. Kristoff didn't care. He had finished!

Anna and Elsa ran over to help him up.

"How did I do?" Kristoff asked. "How long did it take me?"

"Three minutes, forty-eight seconds," Elsa told him.

"Hooray!" cried Olaf.

"Not bad," Kristoff said.

"No, I guess that's not bad. But I did it in three minutes and twenty-seven seconds this morning," Anna said.

"What? You mean you beat me?" he asked.

Anna shrugged. "Elsa did it in three minutes flat."

Kristoff's jaw dropped. He stared at Elsa. She gave him a friendly little wave.

"You look like you could use a hot chocolate," Anna told Kristoff.

"Cold chocolate," he replied. "And a nap."

Chapter 5

A few hours later, Anna and Kristoff were waiting for Elsa in the queen's study.

"I thought we were done training for the day," Kristoff said. They sat down in two comfortable chairs across from Elsa's desk.

"We're done with the physical stuff. Now it's time for the mental stuff," she replied.

"The mental stuff?" asked Kristoff.

"Yes. Part of succeeding in any contest is being able to visualize your goals," Anna told him.

"Visualize. You mean like when I picture having a meat pie for dinner and then I make a meat pie for dinner and eat it?" said Kristoff.

"Sort of," she answered. "Only, this isn't about your stomach—it's about your mind."

A few moments later, Elsa joined them. She sat at her desk and turned to Kristoff. "I heard you have some questions for me," she said.

"I do?" Kristoff said, confused.

"Of course you do," Anna told him. "About the mental stuff."

"The meat pie?" he asked.

"Yes, the meat pie," Anna said encouragingly.

Kristoff turned to Elsa and cleared his throat. "Okay, so I was wondering . . . in a competition where the goal is a . . . meat pie . . . how do I . . . make that pie?"

Elsa looked at him blankly. "Are you asking me for a recipe?" she said, puzzled. "Because you'd have to talk to the chef. I know he uses parsley, but I'm not really sure what else—"

"Not a recipe for meat pies!" Anna interrupted. "A recipe for success!"

Kristoff and Elsa both turned to her. They looked confused.

Anna sighed. "Elsa, you are a *snow*

queen. You can make *snow* and *ice,*" she explained. "Kristoff is in an *ice*-cutting contest. I thought you might have some advice to share with him."

"Oh!" said Elsa. "The whole thing with the pies was really confusing."

"You're telling *me*!" said Kristoff.

"I just thought maybe you could help Kristoff!" Anna said.

"Okay, well, I guess we should start from the beginning," Elsa said. "Kristoff, what's your game plan?"

"To cut ice really fast," he answered simply.

"That sounds pretty solid," Elsa replied.

Anna put her face in her hands. She was thinking of a different kind of advice

for Kristoff. She took a deep breath before looking up again. "As one of his coaches, I just want to make sure he's mentally prepared for the competition," she said. "He already knows how to cut ice, but I don't think he knows how to *be one* with the ice."

Elsa scratched her chin. "I'm not sure I do, either," she said.

"Really?" Anna asked, genuinely surprised. "I thought you had a special connection to ice and snow."

"Well, I do, but I don't quite know how it works," Elsa said thoughtfully. "I guess I'm just so used to it. It's a part of me. I don't think I could explain it."

Anna was quiet for a moment. Even

though Elsa was her sister, she realized there were things she didn't know about her.

"What does it feel like when you use your powers, Elsa?" she asked.

"Like the ice and the snow have given me a gift," Elsa said. "Like they've let me in and said it's okay." The snow queen shrugged. "But mostly, it just feels right."

Anna nodded slowly. Somehow, it made sense—not in her head, but in her heart.

Kristoff cleared his throat gently. "I think I understand," he said. "Cutting ice is a part of me. I've been doing it since I was little."

"Then you have nothing to worry about," Elsa replied with a smile.

Chapter 6

On the morning of the competition, the sun shone brightly over the frozen lake. A large crowd had gathered to watch the contest. Oaken moved his ice engine into position. Kristoff stood with his long saw at the ready.

Anna called them both to the center of the ice. She would be the referee for the match. Elsa would keep time, count ice blocks, and announce the winner.

"Gentlemen, a few ground rules before we begin," Anna said. "You will have ten minutes to cut as many ice blocks as you can. The contestant with the most ice blocks wins. Are we clear?"

Oaken and Kristoff nodded.

"Because this is a friendly competition, there will be no funny business," Anna announced. "That means no illegal tickling, no tweaking of your opponent's nose, and most certainly no snowball throwing. Am I understood?"

"Hoo-hoo! I would like to add a rule," Oaken said.

"What is it?" Anna asked.

"No distracting me with my favorite lingonberry pie," Oaken said.

"And no distracting Oaken with his favorite lingonberry pie," Anna added.

The two men shook hands and returned to their starting positions. Oaken placed Lars the mouse into the metal wheel. Kristoff drew back his saw.

"On your mark, get set, go!" Anna shouted.

Oaken turned the ship's wheel. The ice engine's chain reaction began. The snowshoe kicked the bucket. The bucket spilled the marbles. The marbles ran into the trough. The trough led the marbles to the second bucket. The second bucket sank, raising the cheese above the mouse's wheel. The mouse chased the cheese and spun the wheel. The wheel turned the gears. The gears tripped the lever, opening and closing the coal hatch. The coal spilled into the furnace. Now it was time to wait for the heat to build and the water to boil.

Meanwhile, Kristoff had been sawing steadily. He'd already completed his first block of ice. He knew it would take time for Oaken's machine to heat up. This was his chance. If he could build up a sizable lead, he just might win.

"Two minutes and fifteen seconds!" Elsa called out.

Kristoff pivoted quickly on his feet. He was almost done cutting his second block of ice. He drew the saw swiftly back and forth. Finally, the block broke free. The crowd shouted encouragement. Kristoff grabbed a pair of tongs. He bobbed the ice block down so that it popped up and slid onto the surface of the lake.

A minute or two later, there was a familiar bubbling sound. The water in Oaken's ice engine was about to boil! Oaken rubbed his hands together in anticipation.

Suddenly, the goat horn began to blow. The engine's piston pumped in and out. The flywheel slowly started to turn. The wheel worked the pole with the blade attached to it. Finally, the blade sliced through the ice.

"Five minutes and eleven seconds!" Elsa announced.

Oaken's ice engine roared to life. The blade bobbed up and down on the frozen surface. Within seconds, it had cut its first round ice block.

The crowd of onlookers cheered. They weren't rooting for one side or the other. They just wanted to see a good contest.

Kristoff bobbed his fifth block of ice out of the lake. He glanced over at Oaken, who was leading his invention to a fresh patch of ice. They were halfway through the competition, but Kristoff didn't look tired. In fact, he looked more confident than ever.

Kristoff reached over and picked up

another saw. Now he had one saw in each hand. He slid the blades into the ice, sawing two blocks at once!

"Oooooh," the crowd gasped.

"Seven minutes and thirty seconds!" Elsa said.

Oaken's ice engine was on a roll. It chugged along, churning out one round block of ice after another. Oaken smiled happily, whistling as he led the machine forward on its cart.

Kristoff was breathing heavily. Sawing two blocks at once was a neat trick, but it was also tiring him out faster.

"Ten, nine, eight . . . ," the crowd chanted. They were counting down the last seconds of the competition. Kristoff bobbed his final two blocks of ice from the lake. ". . . five, four, three, two, one!"

Anna blew into a hunter's horn to signal the end of the contest. Elsa hurried over to count the ice blocks. The crowd fell silent, waiting for the official announcement.

Kristoff stood proudly beside his nine blocks of ice. Nine blocks in ten minutes was extraordinary. He was definitely one of the fastest ice harvesters at the lake. Elsa smiled at him as she finished counting. "Great job, Kristoff," she said.

Next, Elsa walked over to the ice engine. There were only six round blocks that Kristoff could see. They were stacked in a row in front of the cart.

Kristoff looked triumphant.

Then Oaken led his cart forward a few paces, revealing what looked like a wall of ice! The cylinders were stacked on top of one another. There were twenty-two in all!

Elsa stepped forward to make the announcement. "The winner is Oaken!" she said. The villagers and the ice harvesters cheered.

Kristoff's face fell. Oaken's machine had won fair and square. Anna and Elsa walked over to him.

"You should be proud, Kristoff," Elsa said. "Look what you've accomplished."

"Yeah," said Anna. "Cutting two blocks at a time! That was incredible."

"Thanks, you two," he said.

Just then, Olaf emerged from the crowd. He bounded up to Kristoff. "Cold hug?" he offered.

Kristoff looked at him and smiled. "Actually, I'll take a warm one, if that's okay," he said, and Olaf hugged him enthusiastically.

Once he had finished hugging Olaf, Kristoff approached Oaken.

"Good job, Oaken," Kristoff said, extending his hand to shake. "I guess maybe a machine *can* be a substitute for a real, live ice harvester."

Oaken shook his head. "My engine is fast, *ja?* It has a lot of parts. It even has a little mouse," he said, petting Lars gently. "But the one thing it does not have is

69

heart." Oaken clapped Kristoff lightly on the shoulder. "I'm hoping we can work together, *ja?* The ice harvesters and the engine."

"I'd like that," Kristoff replied.

"We would, too," said the harvesters,

walking toward them. They congratulated Oaken and praised Kristoff for his impressive ice cutting.

"In fact, we'd love to make you an honorary ice worker, Oaken," Stellan the harvester said. "Bring your engine and meet us at the lake tomorrow morning."

"Hoo-hoo!" Oaken exclaimed. "I'll be there."

Chapter 7

The next morning, Elsa and Anna awoke to chaos in the castle. The chef was very angry. They could hear him banging pots and pans all the way from their rooms. The sisters hurried down to the kitchen to see what was going on.

"I cannot work like this!" the chef complained. His puffy white hat flopped forward over his eyes.

"What's the matter?" Anna asked.

"Spoiled! Everything spoiled! All because there is no ice!" he shouted, pointing to the large icebox he used to keep food fresh. All the vegetables were wilted and the milk had gone sour. The chef usually put a new block of ice in the box each week, but the week's ice hadn't been delivered. "How am I supposed to cook without ingredients?"

"It's okay," Elsa said soothingly. "I'll make you an ice block and you can replace the ingredients."

Elsa concentrated and swirled her hands through the air. Frost gathered at her fingertips. She conjured a large block of ice and guided it into the icebox.

73

"Problem solved," Anna said.

"But the ice delivery?" The chef pouted.

"Elsa and I will investigate," Anna promised. "We'll get to the bottom of it."

Anna and Elsa left the chef, who was already scrambling to make new orders. They stopped in the hall just outside the kitchens.

"It's not like the harvesters to miss a delivery," Anna pointed out.

"I know," Elsa said. "Do you think there's trouble up at the lake?"

"I don't know," Anna said, shrugging. "But today's the day Oaken was going to take his machine there."

Elsa thought for a moment. "If

anything, Oaken's machine should help them harvest *more* ice. It shouldn't cause them to miss a delivery."

Anna nodded. "Unless there was a malfunction?" she suggested.

"Let's pay them a visit," Elsa said.

*

Elsa and Anna rode their horses high into the mountains. When they arrived at the frozen lake, everything looked completely normal—except no one was there.

"That's odd," Elsa said. "The harvesters usually work from sunup to sundown."

"Maybe they are on vacation?" Anna guessed.

"All of them at once?" Elsa replied.

"Yeah, I see what you mean," Anna said. She tried to imagine what could've happened. "Maybe they all got sick?"

"I hope not," Elsa responded.

She and Anna slowly walked across the ice, looking for clues. But they couldn't find anything unusual.

Just then, they heard footsteps behind them. Anna and Elsa turned to see a short, pudgy man with a tremendous hat hurrying toward them. It was Norvald the hatmaker. As usual, he looked worried.

"Your Majesty! My princess! Thank goodness you're here!" Norvald cried. He gripped the brim of his impressive felt hat. A large plume stuck out of the band.

"What's wrong, Norvald?" Elsa asked.

He wrung his hands uneasily. "Oh, it's terrible! Terrible news!" he moaned.

Anna and Elsa exchanged a look. They were concerned, but they also knew that Norvald tended to be overly dramatic. When he was anxious, he imagined the worst possible outcome. People didn't call him Nervous Norvald for nothing.

"Just take a deep breath and tell us what's happened," Anna said calmly.

Norvald squeezed his eyes shut. After a moment, he opened his eyes and began to speak. "This morning, I was walking in the mountains, collecting snowy owl feathers for my latest creation," he said.

"As I drew closer to the frozen lake, I heard shouting."

Norvald explained that he'd overheard an argument, but he couldn't make out all the words. He remembered hearing "ice engine" and "help." Then he'd heard an awful clanging noise. After that, everything fell silent. Norvald could only guess what had happened. He was pretty sure that the ice harvesters had kidnapped Oaken!

Elsa and Anna frowned doubtfully. Norvald's nerves were causing him to jump to wild conclusions. His story was pretty far-fetched.

"Why would they kidnap Oaken?" Elsa asked.

"Well, I heard about the contest yesterday," Norvald said. "I'm sure they were angry that his machine beat them—especially the burly one with the two saws."

"Kristoff? I don't see Kristoff leading a kidnapping plot," Anna said.

"Me either," Elsa responded. "Kristoff and the ice harvesters would never kidnap anyone! Maybe you misunderstood?"

"Maybe," Norvald answered hesitantly. He looked thoughtful for a moment. "Oh no!"

"What?" Anna and Elsa asked.

"Well, I was just thinking, if the harvesters didn't kidnap Oaken, maybe someone kidnapped *them*!" Norvald cried.

"Who would kidnap Oaken and all of the ice harvesters?" Elsa questioned.

"AN ABOMINABLE SNOWMAN!" Norvald shouted fearfully.

"I . . . don't think that's possible," Elsa said politely. She knew that Norvald was trying to help. But he was too nervous to think clearly.

"Then how do you explain this?" he asked. He pulled a torn scrap of paper from his pocket. He'd found it on the ice after the argument. Written on the paper in shaky handwriting was *help*!

Elsa and Anna looked at the scrap of paper. They weren't sure what it meant, but they knew it had nothing to do with abominable snowmen.

"Maybe they went to get help for something?" Anna said to Elsa.

Elsa nodded. "That seems reasonable. Why don't we follow their tracks and make sure they're okay?"

"Good idea," Anna replied.

Norvald breathed a sigh of relief.

"That's wonderful news, Your Majesty. I know you'll be able to save them!"

Anna wasn't so sure anyone needed saving, but she and Elsa were ready . . . just in case.

Chapter 8

After gathering food and supplies in the village, Anna and Elsa returned to the mountains. They found footprints and other tracks leading away from the frozen lake.

"Are those wheel ruts?" Anna asked, pointing to ground.

Elsa knelt to examine them. "I think

so," she said. "Maybe they were made by the ice engine's cart."

Elsa and Anna climbed onto their horses. They followed the tracks toward the snowy woods. They'd only been riding a few minutes when Olaf bounded into view. He waved happily.

"Olaf, what are you doing here?" Anna asked.

"I'm heading to the lake. It's Oaken's first day as an ice harvester, and I want to see him work the engine thingy," Olaf said brightly.

"I'm afraid you're too late, Olaf. Oaken and the harvesters aren't there," Elsa explained.

"Where did they go?" Olaf asked.

"We don't know," Anna said. "But we're riding after them to make sure they're okay."

"Why wouldn't they be okay?"

Elsa and Anna exchanged a glance. They didn't want to worry Olaf, but they knew they should tell him the truth. Anna showed him the torn slip of paper Norvald had given them. Olaf stared at it. Then a huge smile spread across his face.

"They want us to help with the feast!" he said.

Elsa looked at him, puzzled.

"What feast?" Anna asked.

"The 'Welcome, Oaken!' feast!" Olaf answered.

"We didn't hear anything about a feast," Elsa said.

"Oh, I didn't either," said Olaf. "But I'm sure there is one. Cutting ice is hard work. It makes people hungry."

"Olaf, you think the ice harvesters missed an ice delivery and took off in the middle of the day to go have a feast with Oaken?" Elsa asked.

"Not just any feast—a delicious welcome feast," Olaf said, smiling.

"And they left us a note asking for help?" asked Anna. "How could we help with a feast?"

"Hmm," Olaf said, considering this. "Maybe they want us to deliver ice while they eat?"

Elsa raised an eyebrow. The harvesters wouldn't ask anyone else to deliver ice. It was their job.

She and Anna decided to keep searching. Olaf joined them. The three friends followed the tracks through the woods. The footprints led between the tall trees covered with snow. Anna paid special attention to the wagon tracks that marked the engine's path. Eventually, the wheel ruts led into a clearing.

"Look!" Elsa said, pointing. In the center of the clearing was a ring of stones with a pile of burned branches inside. "There was a campfire here."

Anna walked over to the stones. She held her hand above the pile of branches and twigs. It was still warm. She knew that the harvesters must have been there recently. "We're on the right path," she said.

Olaf bounced up and down excitedly. "We're on the right path to the feast!"

Anna, Elsa, and Olaf followed the tracks out of the clearing and onto a narrow path. The path wound through the trees and down into a wide, snow-covered field. By the time they crossed the field, the sun had begun to set.

The search had taken much longer than Anna had expected. It was getting dark, and they still hadn't found Oaken and the ice harvesters.

"Maybe we should make camp now," she said.

Elsa nodded in agreement.

"I love camping!" Olaf said eagerly. "What's camping?"

Elsa explained that camping was what people did when the slept outdoors. She and Anna did what they thought campers would do. First, the sisters found water for the horses. They tied their reins to a nearby tree. Then Anna looked at Elsa expectantly. She'd never been camping before. She hoped her older sister would take the lead.

But Elsa just stared back. They had both grown up in a castle. They'd never had to spend the night in the woods.

"I guess we need a campfire?" Elsa said.

"Right," Anna replied.

They gathered small pieces of wood and set them in a pile. Anna and Elsa looked at the pile. Neither one made a move.

"How are we going to light this?" Elsa asked.

"You're the magical one," Anna said lightheartedly.

"Then it looks like we've got a problem," Elsa replied. Her ability to conjure snow and ice wasn't helpful in this situation.

"Oooh, can we roast marshmallows?" Olaf piped up. He didn't seem to mind that no one knew how to light the fire.

"I don't think *you* should roast anything," Anna said gently. Elsa had given Olaf a little snow cloud that kept him from melting in the heat. But roasting marshmallows over an open fire seemed like too much of a risk.

The problem remained. They didn't know how to make a fire.

"If we don't have a fire, how will we keep warm?" Anna asked. The wind was picking up. It was getting colder as night fell.

"Warm hugs?" Olaf suggested.

*

Unfortunately, Olaf's hugs weren't enough to keep Anna warm. It grew colder as the night wore on. Eventually, it began to snow.

Elsa didn't mind the cold, but Anna

93

was beginning to shiver. Elsa looked at her sister with concern. Then she swirled her hands in front of her. Elsa traced her fingers through the air and conjured blocks of ice. She guided the blocks into a huge mound. Then she arranged the blocks carefully and rounded the edges.

An enormous shelter formed in front of Anna's eyes. "Elsa, it's an igloo!" she breathed in amazement.

Elsa nodded. She finished building the ice hut and led Anna and Olaf inside.

"It's warm in here," said Anna, brushing the snow from her dress and hair.

"Warmer than outside, at least," Elsa explained. "It'll keep us out of the snow."

The igloo was big enough for the horses,

too. They led the animals inside. Elsa pulled two blankets from the saddlebags and gave them to Anna. Anna wrapped herself up tight and huddled close to her sister.

Outside, the wind howled and the snow fell. But inside the igloo, everyone was safe and warm.

Chapter 9

The next morning, Olaf was the first to peek outside. The snow had stopped, the sky was clear, and the ground was coated in a fresh layer of snow. Olaf sighed contentedly. "I love newly fallen snow!" he exclaimed.

Anna and Elsa were not so happy to see the snow. As they climbed onto their horses, they realized that the ice harvester's tracks had been lost! The new snow had covered them during the night!

"What should we do, Elsa?" Anna asked. She knew they could turn around and go back to the castle. But that wouldn't solve anything if the harvesters really needed their help.

"I'm not sure." Elsa said. "If you were an ice harvester, where would you go?" she asked.

Anna considered her sister's question. She thought about the ice harvester she knew best—Kristoff. Anna tried to think like him. Kristoff was always pretending to talk for his reindeer, Sven.

Anna thought maybe if she pretended to speak for Kristoff, it would help her figure things out. *"Hello, I'm Kristoff. I like to cut ice and wax my sled,"* she said.

"Anna, are you feeling all right?" Elsa asked.

"I'm fine," Anna answered. "I'm just thinking like an ice harvester."

"You're talking like one, too!" Olaf pointed out cheerfully.

Anna imagined what it was like to be Kristoff. If he was traveling with Oaken and the other harvesters, what would he do? He'd certainly help make camp. Kristoff had been raised in the woods, so he was a camping expert.

He'd also have to take care of Sven. They always traveled together. Kristoff usually kept carrots with him. Carrots were Sven's favorite food.

"Are there any towns nearby?" Anna asked.

Elsa studied their surroundings. She pictured the maps at home in her study. She often looked at them to plan journeys to neighboring kingdoms. "I think we're close to Jorgen's Forge," she said.

Anna had heard of Jorgen's Forge. It was a town known for its blacksmiths—men and women who made things out of metal. "Are you thinking what I'm thinking?" she asked her sister.

Elsa nodded. "It makes sense. Maybe Oaken wanted to have the blacksmiths make a part for his machine."

"Elsa, do you think you can get us to Jorgen's Forge from here?" Anna asked.

"I'll do my best," Elsa said. She looked to her left and then right. After a moment, she set off into the trees. Anna followed, and Olaf bounded happily after them.

*

Two hours later, Anna, Elsa, and Olaf were still traveling through the snowy woods.

"Do you know where we are, Elsa?" Anna asked. "It feels like we're going around in circles."

Elsa stopped and looked for a landmark.

Nearby she spotted a huge rock. She recognized it from one of the maps. "That's the Hopping Rock," she said, pointing to the large snow-covered stone. "It's on the way to Jorgen's Forge."

"Why do they call it the Hopping Rock?" Olaf asked.

"Legend has it that the rock is enchanted. They say it hops from place to place," Elsa answered.

"I hope it doesn't really hop," Anna said. "If it does, how can we know where we are?"

"Good question," Elsa replied. If there was any truth to the legend, they might be on the wrong path.

"Why don't we take a break and I'll

scout ahead," Elsa said. "I'll make sure we're on the right track."

Elsa and Anna got down from their horses. Anna thought it might be a good time for a snack. She took some bread and cheese from her saddlebag while Elsa walked farther into the woods.

Anna walked over to the Hopping Rock. She brushed the snow aside and sat down to eat her bread. As she did, she noticed something odd a few feet behind the rock. There was a trail of orange crumbs.

Curious, Anna stood and walked over to the trail. She knelt to examine the crumbs. As she looked closer, she saw that they weren't crumbs. They were tiny

pieces of carrot. *Who would leave a trail of carrots in the middle of the woods?* Anna thought.

Just then, Anna remembered. Sven loved carrots. She also knew that Kristoff had called Sven a messy eater.

"Elsa! Olaf! Come quickly!" Anna called.

Elsa came running through the trees.

She and the snowman hurried over to the Hopping Rock.

"Look!" Anna said. "I think Sven accidentally left us a trail!"

"Are those carrots?" Elsa asked.

"Yes!" Anna answered. "I think the harvesters went this way."

"Let's follow the trail!" Elsa said.

The sisters climbed onto their horses. Olaf bounded up into the saddle with Anna. The three friends began to ride.

"I've always wanted to follow a trail of crumbs!" Olaf exclaimed. "It's just like in a fairy tale!"

Chapter 10

A while later, Elsa, Anna, and Olaf rode into Jorgen's Forge. The trail of carrot pieces led directly to a large barn in the center of town. Anna could hear loud clanging and banging coming from inside.

"I guess this is the place," Anna said to Elsa and Olaf. She knocked on the barn door and waited. A couple of minutes passed and no one answered.

"Maybe they can't hear us over the noise," Elsa said. She pushed on the door and it creaked open. A blast of heat came from inside. Olaf's cloud hovered over his head and snowed gently to keep him cold.

Anna, Elsa, and Olaf stepped into the barn. It was a huge space with wooden beams running across a high ceiling. Fires burned in special pits in each corner of the room. Beside each fire was a blacksmith. The blacksmiths heated metal over their fires. When the metal got hot enough, they could beat it into any shape with a hammer.

"Wow!" Olaf exclaimed, watching the blacksmiths work.

Anna looked around the barn. She

spotted Oaken, Kristoff, Sven, and the other ice harvesters huddled in the center. At that moment, Kristoff looked up. Surprised, he walked over to Anna.

"What are you all doing here?" he asked.

"We could ask you the same thing," Anna replied.

"Didn't you get our note?" said Kristoff.

"You mean this?" Anna responded, taking the scrap of paper from her pocket.

"Oh," Kristoff said. "This is all that was left? It looks like something chewed on it."

"Norvald found it," Elsa explained. "He thought you'd been kidnapped."

"Leave it to Nervous Norvald to imagine a kidnapping," Kristoff said good-naturedly. "Is that why you're here? To rescue us?"

"We just thought we should make sure everything was okay," Anna told him. "After all, it's not every day that the ice harvesters miss a delivery and disappear."

"Yeah, well, I guess we have some explaining to do," Kristoff said.

He told Anna, Elsa, and Olaf the story of Oaken's first day as an honorary ice harvester. Everything had started off normally. Oaken got his ice engine up and running. He showed each of the harvesters how to run the machine. There was just

one problem. With the engine running so much, Lars was getting tired. Oaken didn't design the machine to run from sunup to sundown.

Everyone loved Lars, and they wanted him to rest. So Oaken and the ice harvesters thought of ways they could run the engine without the mouse.

"We all got really excited about it," Kristoff said. "People were shouting out ideas left and right."

"That must have been what Norvald overheard," Elsa said. "He thought there was an argument."

"An argument? No, just a bunch of passionate ice workers talking at once," Kristoff explained. "A few of the harvesters started tinkering around with the machine. Unfortunately, one of the gear teeth broke."

Kristoff said that Oaken had decided to go to Jorgen's Forge for a replacement gear. He wanted to take a few of the harvesters with him, but everyone wanted to go! They were eager to help Oaken make improvements. They left a note saying that they'd gone to get help with the machine. No one thought the trip would take more than a couple of hours. But with such a large group, traveling took longer than expected. The harvesters missed their ice delivery!

"And we still haven't fixed the machine," Kristoff said.

"What do you mean?" Elsa asked. "What about the gear?"

"Oh, Brigida made us a new gear, but Oaken thought we should make all the improvements at once," Kristoff explained.

"Brigida?" asked Anna.

"Our blacksmith," Kristoff answered. "I'll introduce you."

Kristoff took Anna, Elsa, and Olaf into the huddle of ice harvesters. Brigida the blacksmith stood talking to Oaken. She wore a heavy leather apron and held a large hammer.

Brigida greeted Anna, Elsa, and Olaf with a friendly smile.

"Wow, look at your hammer!" Olaf said. "Can I hold it?"

"I don't know. It's pretty heavy," Brigida replied.

"Please?" Olaf begged.

Brigida leaned down and handed her hammer to Olaf. It slipped right through his stick fingers and landed on the ground with a thud.

Oaken was happy to see Anna, Elsa, and Olaf. "Hoo-hoo!" he greeted them. "So glad to see you, friends. Maybe you can help us with a little dilemma."

"We'll try," Elsa said.

Oaken showed them the changes he'd made to the ice engine. He'd removed the ship's wheel, the buckets, the marbles, the pulley, the goat horn, and the mouse's wheel. The machine was a lot smaller than before. It looked easier to use.

Anna noticed that the blade was different, too—there was a round saw, like a jagged wheel, in the front of the cart.

"That was my idea," Brigida said. "It will cut straight lines instead of round ones."

"Round blocks are interesting," Kristoff explained. "But straight lines waste less ice."

"That's great. So what's the problem?" Anna asked.

"Without the mouse's wheel, there is nothing to turn the gears, *ja?*" Oaken said. "The gears work the lever, and the lever works the coal hatch. How are we to drop the coal slowly into the chute?"

"Good question," Elsa said. She and Anna stared at the ice engine. They walked around the cart and looked at it from every angle. Suddenly, Anna had an idea.

"Elsa! The Cat-a-Cleaner!" she said, thinking back to their childhood invention.

"What do you mean, Anna?" Elsa asked.

"What if we build a catapult? Instead of the gears and the lever and the coal hatch, what if we sling the coal directly into the chute?"

Elsa thought it over. "You mean the harvesters could take turns launching the coal?"

"Well, it's certainly easier than sawing through ice," Anna replied.

"Hoo-hoo! That's a wonderful idea," Oaken said. Kristoff and the other harvesters agreed.

Brigida offered to build the catapult with Anna and Elsa. They were happy to accept her helping hand and hammer.

✳

Later, Elsa, Anna, Olaf and the ice harvesters went back to the frozen lake. Everyone was excited to test Oaken's new and improved ice engine. The contraption was still on a horse-drawn cart. But without its wheels, buckets, and gears, the machine looked different. Only the food tin, furnace, flywheel, and cutting blade remained. Also, next to the cart was a small catapult made of iron and wood.

"This is so exciting!" Olaf said, hopping up and down eagerly.

Oaken wanted Anna and Elsa to be the first to try the new engine. Since they'd helped to make the catapult, he thought it was only fair.

"Hoo-hoo! Whenever you're ready," he said to the sisters.

Elsa and Anna walked over to the catapult. Kristoff slid a large barrel of coal into place beside them.

"Good luck," he said.

Anna drew back the catapult's arm. It had a small cup at the end to hold the coal. She placed a lump of coal into the cup. Then she fastened the arm in place with rope.

"Okay, on the count of three," Elsa said. She began to count. The crowd of ice harvesters counted along with her. "One . . . two . . . *three*!"

Anna pulled the rope and released the arm. It sprang forward. The lump of coal flew through the air. It landed in the open chute and fell into the furnace.

"Hooray!" the crowd cheered.

Anna quickly reset the arm so that Elsa could launch the next piece of coal. She loaded the coal into the cup and pulled the rope.

"Bull's-eye!" Anna said as Elsa's coal fell down the chute.

After a couple of minutes, everyone heard the familiar bubbling sound. The water was boiling in the food tin. Soon steam blew through the hole in the top of

119

the tin where the goat horn used to be. Now the machine whistled like a teakettle. The piston in the tin pumped in and out. Slowly, the flywheel started to turn, and the round saw blade sliced the ice.

Another cheer rose from the crowd. The first block had been cut! Oaken led the cart to a fresh patch of ice.

A short while later, Elsa and Anna stared at the long row of ice blocks stretched out behind them.

Oaken was the first to thank them. "Hoo-hoo, ladies!" he said. "I couldn't have done this without you." Lars the mouse squeaked happily from the pocket of his sweater.

"*You* did it, Oaken," Elsa pointed out. "We just made a little fix."

Oaken shook his head. "It is not so. You have laid the foundation for the future of ice harvesting!" he exclaimed. He hugged Anna and Elsa warmly. Then he climbed into the cart to inspect the catapult.

"Do you think this is really the future of ice harvesting?" Anna asked Kristoff when he walked over to the two of them.

Kristoff shrugged. "It's definitely an advance. But I think we'll keep our saws around a little longer," he said lightly.

Anna and Elsa said goodbye to Kristoff. They linked arms and started the long walk back to town.

After a few minutes, Anna said, "Do you think those engines will ever replace the harvesters?"

"I don't see how," Elsa said. "Oaken's engine still needs people to run it."

"I know. I was just thinking about what Kristoff said about there being no substitute for a real, live ice harvester."

"I think he's right," Elsa told her. "Some things are irreplaceable."

Anna looked at Elsa and smiled. "Like sisters?" she asked.

"Exactly," Elsa replied. "Sisters are one of a kind."

© Jenn Carvin Photography

Erica David has written more than forty books and comics for young readers, including Marvel Adventures *Spider-Man: The Sinister Six.* She graduated from Princeton University and is an MFA candidate at the Writer's Foundry in Brooklyn. She has always had an interest in all things magical, fantastic, and frozen, which has led her to work for Nickelodeon, Marvel, and an ice cream parlor, respectively. She resides sometimes in Philadelphia and sometimes in New York, with a canine familiar named Skylar.